FRIDAY THE 13TH

by Steven Kroll

illustrated by Dick Gackenbach

HOLIDAY HOUSE　　　　　*NEW YORK*

Text copyright © 1981 by Steven Kroll
Illustrations copyright © 1981 by Dick Gackenbach
Printed in the United States of America

Library of Congress Cataloging in Publication Data

Kroll, Steven
  Friday the 13th.

  SUMMARY: Unlucky Harold, for whom every day is Friday
the 13th, finally has a change of fortune.
  [1. Luck—Fiction] I. Gackenbach, Dick. II. Title.
PZ7.K9225Fr   [E]   80-28769
ISBN 0-8234-0392-0

For my mother, umpire extraordinary

Nothing ever went right for Harold.

And his sister Hilda never let him forget it.

Every morning, when Harold ate breakfast, he spilled egg on his shirt. And every morning, clean little Hilda said, "Look at piggy Harold!"

Every time Harold went to play soccer, it rained. And every time, dry little Hilda said, "Ha, ha! It's too wet to play, boys!"

Every night, when
Harold washed the dishes,
he broke one.
And every night, sweet
little Hilda said, "For you,
Harold, every day is
Friday the 13th!"

Harold was sure this was true, and when Friday the 13th came, he just knew it was going to be the worst day ever.

And he was right.

When he looked in his bureau drawer, none of his clothes went together. So when he came down the stairs, Hilda sang, "Look at Harold's funny clothes!"

On the way to school, the school bus came to a
sudden stop. Harold spilled all his pencils and crayons,
and Hilda shouted, "Clumsy Harold! Clumsy Harold!"

At school, Harold skinned his knee during recess. "Harold can't do anything right!" Hilda said to everyone.

By lunchtime, Harold was miserable. So when he opened his lunch box and found an egg salad sandwich, he almost burst into tears. He hated egg salad, and Hilda had a peanut butter and jelly sandwich, his favorite kind.

All Harold wanted to do was go home. But he couldn't. He was an outfielder on the Middletown Knights, the school softball team. Even though he almost never got to play, he had to be at the games. That afternoon the Knights were going to play the Main Street Badgers.

No one wanted to play the game on Friday the 13th. Everyone was sure terrible things were going to happen.

And they were right.

Before the game, Alex, the Knights' shortstop, got sick to his stomach. Coach Redfield looked down at his bench. Two other players were out sick. Only Harold was left.

"But I can't play shortstop!" said Harold.

"Just do the best you can," said Coach Redfield.

The Knights' fans cheered as Harold took the field. Three times the ball was hit to him, and three times he missed it. The cheers quickly turned to boos.

"That's my clumsy brother, Harold!" Hilda shouted from the grandstand.

Harold turned very red.

In the third inning, he came up to bat and struck out.

"Dummy!" someone shouted.

"You must be blind, Harold!" Hilda joined in.

Harold walked sadly back to the sidelines.

By the seventh inning, the score was five to four. The Badgers were winning. It was their last time up at bat.

Their biggest slugger hit a ground ball to Harold. He caught it, and dropped it. The Badgers scored another run.

"Boo!" yelled the crowd.

"Get him out of there!" shouted Hilda.

Harold felt like crawling into a hole somewhere. But he couldn't. He had to finish the game.

The Badgers made three quick outs, and the Knights were up. When Harold came to bat, there were two outs and runners on first and second base.

It was the last chance for the Middletown Knights, so instead of booing Harold as usual, the Knights' fans went back to cheering him.

"Come on, Harold!" they shouted. "Get something going!"

Hilda, of course, said nothing.

Harold swung on the first pitch and missed. He swung on the second pitch and missed.

"Come on, Harold!" the fans shouted again. "Hit one out of here!"

And that's exactly what Harold did. He felt himself fill with confidence. He swung on the next pitch and hit a home run.

At first, he didn't realize what had happened. He stood at home plate, wondering where the ball had gone.

"Run!" someone shouted. "Run!"

And someone else started pushing him toward first base.

Finally Harold understood. He began circling the bases. The crowd went wild. He felt wonderful. The Knights had won, seven runs to six!

His teammates lifted him onto their shoulders, shouting "Hooray for Harold!" He was the hero, and he had never felt so good, Friday the 13th or not.

Starting home, with Hilda nowhere to be seen,
Harold whistled happily. Halfway there, it began to rain.

Harold held up his hand. "I guess this is a Friday
the 13th rain," he said out loud. "But it's a very nice, soft
rain, and I don't really mind it at all."

He didn't run. He kept on walking.
One block from his house, a car splashed
him with mud.

Hilda popped out from behind a tree.
"Harold is a mess!" she sang, and dashed away.

Harold was fed up. "Cut it out, Hilda!" he shouted after her. "Enough's enough."

He brushed the mud off his clothes. There were only a few spots. He was sure they'd come out in the laundry.

Harold started whistling again as he reached his house. He went into the kitchen and got some juice and a piece of cake. Before he could take a sip of juice, he dropped his glass.

Hilda stuck her head in the door. "Slobby Harold," she said. "Clumsy, slobby Harold!"

Hilda slipped in the puddle of juice and knocked over the kitchen table.

The rest of the cake fell on her head. Harold burst out laughing.

He looked down at angry, soggy Hilda.
"Happy Friday the 13th, Hilda!" he said.